C

About the Author
The Gift of the O

The Houseplant	1
The Houseplant Merch	19
Enjoyed the Houseplant?	21
Also By	23
Words From the Author	25
Bonus	27
Contacting Author	29
Acknowledgments	31

About the Author

Jeremy Ray graduated from Carnegie Mellon University with a MFA in Dramatic Writing. He is the recipient of the Max K. Lerner Playwriting Fellowship for his play *Boiling Point* and the Shubert Playwriting Fellowship for his play *Sisters of Transformation*. His work has been performed at the Kennedy Center in Washington DC, and his screenplays have placed in the PAGE International Screenwriting Awards Competition, The Academy Nicholl Fellowship, and the ScreenCraft Drama Contest.

However, he is most fond of prose. He spends

his free time devouring books like the bookworm he is. You can go here to find out what he's currently reading:

www.goodreads.com/jeremyraystories

∼

Enjoy audiobooks, podcasts, both? Every week you can find him on the *Nobody Reads Short Stories* podcast presenting a new short story (all genres) from a diverse assortment of authors. You can find it here:

www.nobodyreadsshortstories.com

Copyright © 2020 by Jeremy Ray
All rights reserved.
www.jeremyraystories.com

Cover design by Lance Buckley

No part of this book may be reproduced or used in any manner without the written permission of the copyright owner except for the use of quotations in a book review.

For any inquiries regarding this book, please email:
info@jeremyraystories.com

As an author, I am reader-supported. When you purchase through my links, I may earn an affiliate commission. This means I will earn a small percentage on sales with no extra cost to you, and sometimes you might even get a discount from using my links. (Yay team!) I only recommend products I appreciate & enjoy or have created myself. That won't ever change. I value honesty, so you'll always know exactly what I think of something.

This story is a work of fiction. Names, characters, places, and incidents either are the product of the author's imagination or are used fictitiously. Any resemblance to actual persons, living or dead, events, or locales is entirely coincidental.

Growing up, I was a big fan of how Pixar would put short films in front of their features. The following micro-story is my way of doing the same.

The Gift of the Only Ones

A MICRO-STORY BY JEREMY RAY

The leafy plant waited in anticipation
to have its flower heads bloom.
It wanted to know what kind of flower
in the garden it would turn into.
Would it be a white rose,
a red tulip, a pink hyacinth,
or a purple crocus? All great choices!

When yellow petals bloomed,
it realized it was none of these flowers in the garden.
It decided it must be special since it was the only one.

When the time came,
the dandelion released its white seeds
to fly into the air. It wanted to give other gardens
the gift of the only ones.

My subscribers get a brand new micro-story delivered to their email every week — FREE! To join, go here:

landing.jeremyraystories.com/microstory

THE HOUSEPLANT

A Short Story

JEREMY RAY

Infinite Ray Publishing

Dedication and About The Story

Years ago, I did not have a green thumb and avoided getting plants of my own. I worried that any plant I purchased would meet a horrible end. My former roommate had a ton of plants, one of which he never watered. It was in our bathroom and it was hard watching it slowly turning brown from lack of care. Eventually I watered it myself. A bond grew. When I moved out, I offered my roommate money for it, but we were not on the best terms and he refused.

I wonder what happened to my green friend. It hurts imagining it there, waiting for me to return and water it again. But I hope for the best. I hope my roommate started watering it and it's still alive and thriving.

I dedicate this short story to the plant I left behind, and to my own fern, Benjie.

The Houseplant

BY JEREMY RAY

❦

The houseplant loved Sundays because Brenda hosted her women's book club in the reading room. The women would sit at the long table, next to the plant's window, and discuss chapters of the book they were reading. The houseplant liked the energy vibrations released when these humans produced their laughter; however, it most enjoyed when the woman-humans were done with the discussion because that's when they would turn and admire the houseplant's beauty. Sundays in the reading room became a compliment extravaganza, especially when new members who had never seen the houseplant before came, like the two new women this Sunday, who by complimenting the houseplant, had spurred Brenda onto a story she had told many times before:

"Me and George met three years ago..." The women weren't the only ones listening to Brenda's story. Over the years, the fern had become a skilled expert at human language, and its expertise went beyond the mere words themselves into their finer nuances. It could smell and taste the subtle chemical changes humans released while producing the words. And it felt the subtle vibrational shifts in how the words themselves were being conveyed. On top of that, it could see the electrical signals being transmitted through the entire human body. The houseplant had come a long way in understanding humankind and prided itself in often understanding humans better than they understood themselves. While the woman-humans toiled away with the meaning of Brenda's words, the plant just knew. Humans call this knowing "intuition" because they use it so infrequently.

If Brenda had been using *her* intuition, she would have known that the regular members of the book club, though they loved her dearly, were secretly bored to death with the houseplant story. They had heard it so many times before. But because of their love for Brenda, they presented their most cordial smiles as Brenda turned to the two new women, engrossed in her own story of how she met the houseplant.

"I was in line at Garden Palace — have no idea what I was buying — doesn't even matter — anyway, I felt someone tapping me on my rear end. Well, I turned around and was just about to let the guy behind me have it, when I noticed that it wasn't the man — it was this tiny fern trying to get my attention." Brenda stroked one of the houseplant's leaves as she spoke. "I looked down at him and it was love at first sight. Right, George?"

Wrong. This was not the real story. It might have been "love at first sight" for Brenda, but it was certainly not for the houseplant. Brenda's backside kept infringing on its territory. If the plant could have moved away, it would have. This kind of harassment was typical for the plants placed on the display table next to the aisles in Garden Palace.

THE HOUSEPLANT

The fern had yearned to be placed back in its original position: in the middle of the houseplants, away from all the humans. There, it had enjoyed listening to the sound waves of its neighboring plants, and felt a particular fondness for a neighboring palm tree. The fern, for months, had been moving its roots over to the side of the pot closest to the palm tree, in hopes of one day being able to entwine with its friend. But that time never came. What did come were the fat-filled human backsides.

There was no contentment for the plants on the outer edges of the display table, especially in May when the buying frenzy would reach a fever pitch. The plants would watch in trepidation as their dear friends were taken. The most dangerous place for a houseplant was the corner of the table nearest the checkout lane, reserved only for the most beautiful of plants. The plants considered this Danger-Corner. There, the plants suffered the most human abuses. They were picked up as often as they were knocked over. Even more cruel were the humans' tiny offspring, who frequently ripped off flowers and leaves from the beautiful plants. But the fern never imagined that it would have to worry. It thought it would remain safe in the middle of the table, forever: it was ugly.

The fern had been at Garden Palace so long that it understood that the plants that attracted the most attention were the ones humans found aesthetically pleasing. It had seen it time and time again over the years; beautiful plants just didn't have a chance. The Purple Orchid, who had been in Danger-Corner right before the houseplant, was the perfect example. Each time the orchid had been lifted by a human, it did what scared plants do: it released warning chemicals into the air. The first few days this defense mechanism had worked for the orchid. The human picker-uppers had intuitively put the orchid back down, but because intuition comes to humans in whispers, none of them knew exactly why. Instead, to help them understand their feelings, they came up with excuses. The fat-man-human had mumbled that the orchid was "too big," the gay-man-human had turned to his partner and said, "It doesn't match our drapes," and the old-woman-human had thought to herself, "Not for me. Orchids are too hard to care for."

But then the tall, thin-woman-human came and picked the orchid up. "She's so beautiful, I must have her," the woman mumbled.

The Purple Orchid had sprayed its volatiles into the air in hopes of being put down. And the woman had hesitated: "Should I think about this first, come back later?" she said to herself. "No. She's too beautiful, someone else will take her." And just like that, the orchid was gone.

But because the fern knew what humans considered beautiful, it had skillfully remained the opposite for years. It stunted its own growth and kept its leaves shriveled up like a head of lettuce. The strategy worked brilliantly. It was why the fern had remained at Garden Palace years longer than any of the other plants. It always went unnoticed by customers and Garden Palace workers alike, and that's how it would always remain, or so the fern thought.

Ultimately the fern's self-imposed homeliness was also its undoing. A new Garden Palace employee had taken pity on the "poor ugly dude" and intentionally replaced the empty spot left behind by the beautiful orchid with the fern, in hopes of getting the houseplant sold. Even after being

THE HOUSEPLANT

moved, the ugly fern thought it was safe — until Brenda's rear end attacked.

"He was just screaming to be taken," Brenda cooed to her book club.

Not true. The houseplant screamed with its volatiles to be set back down. It kept screaming when she put it in her cart, and practically screeched when Brenda put it into her passenger seat. It kept doing so the whole drive home.

The fern only stopped screaming once Brenda parked in the garage and opened her car door, because it sensed that it was not alone. It smelled all the plants of the neighborhood — the grass, the flowers, the giant oak tree. The fern had thought maybe it had been wrong to be scared of Brenda. Maybe she would plant it outside in the earth!

Oh, how it had always dreamed to be planted in the ground where it could really be connected to other plants! The fern's roots would be colonized by the thin threads of fungi known as mycelium that would link the fern's roots to all the other plants of the neighborhood. It would merely have to secrete a few tiny chemical signals through its roots to be able to communicate to plants far and wide!

But then Brenda pressed a button and the garage door lowered on the fern's hopes and dreams. It was left with fake light, and Brenda.

"You're home now," Brenda said as she hoisted the fern into her arms.

She brought the fern inside, and the plant immediately used all its senses to search the place for any other plants. There were none, in any of the rooms Brenda walked through. What it did sense were other humans. Dread took over as a large man-human came out of one of the rooms. Brenda held up the fern like an offering for man-human to examine. Was the man-human going to rip it out by the roots while she watched in delight?

The plant felt vibrations as a girl-human and a younger boy-human raced down the steps to see what their mother was holding. The boy-human reached up and grabbed onto one of the fern's leaves, and the plant screamed louder than it had ever screamed before; it had witnessed enough at Garden Palace to know that human children were the most vicious of creatures.

"Be careful, you don't want to rip the leaves out," Brenda said as she knelt down for the boy-offspring to take a better look.

"Can I have it?" asked little boy-offspring.

The girl-offspring snickered. "Yeah, give it to him, you're just going to kill it like all the others anyway."

"Dead plant walking," said the man-human. Girl-offspring and man-human cackled.

"Ha ha, real funny," laughed Brenda as she stood up again.

Was Brenda really a plant killer?

As if to answer, Brenda climbed up the same stairs the little humans had come down from and placed the fern in a bathroom. A glass vase of wilting roses on the sink confirmed all the fern's worst fears. It sensed the volatiles coming from the roses that translated to: "Help me, I'm dying, I'm dying."

So, the plant deduced, *this is the torture chamber where Brenda brings plants to murder*. There was plenty of moisture in the air, but no sunlight. And if that wasn't horrible enough, Brenda overwatered, so the fern struggled to breathe. The plant began to wilt. The more it wilted, the more she watered.

It became apparent she was *trying* to drown it. But the fern was determined to triumph, and when Brenda threw the dead roses into the wastebasket (they had stopped communicating days before), it resolved that it would not be another victim of this cruel mistress.

It would be the plant that lived.

And it did. The fern clung to life for weeks in that bathroom, even when it seemed all hope was lost. Then one morning, Brenda came into the bathroom, looked down at the wilting fern, and sighed. The plant sensed her frustration and assumed she was frustrated it had survived. Brenda grabbed the fern and placed it on the balcony where there was plenty of sunlight and moisture, and the fern could hear, smell, feel the fellow plants in the neighborhood again. It had defeated the human, and this was the victory it deserved. Or so it thought, until the sun rose. There was no protection from the fierce rays, and the fern's fronds began to cook at the tips. The fern felt searing pain as the charring slowly moved up its fronds.

So Brenda has a new plan, it occurred to the plant: *burn me alive*. The fern dispatched warning signals to the plants below the balcony, in the neighborhood gardens. Translated, the signals screamed: "Evil woman tortures plants — grow away from here!"

To Brenda's credit, she did bring the houseplant into the shady reading room the moment she got home from work and saw the fern's blackened fronds.

"I'm sorry," she said.

When she touched the leaves, inspecting the damage she had caused, the plant could sense through the contact that Brenda felt regret for the injuries. But so what? She hadn't been killing it on purpose; this didn't change the fact that she was incompetent and should never have any plants, ever.

As time went by, it became harder for the plant to hold onto its grudge. Brenda tried to improve, and did. She learned how to properly care for the fern, spraying it on a daily basis. She even placed a pan of wet pebbles under the houseplant's pot so that humidity was constantly in the air for it to quench its thirst whenever it wanted. The fern turned green again, and the joy this brought Brenda complicated the plant's feelings further.

The plant associated the feeling of joy with predators. It had witnessed that feeling mostly when a predator conquered its prey. When bugs felt joy around plants, it was because they were about to eat them. When humans felt joy around plants, it was because they were about to conquer them. So Brenda's joy seemed like a display of dominance.

So what did the fern do? It stifled its growth, curling up its leaves and turning itself into the shape of a cabbage once again, this time in rebellion. *Just let her try and turn me beautiful*, it thought. It prided itself in becoming even more hideous than it had been at Garden Palace. That would show Brenda who was dominant!

But Brenda's joy didn't go away; she didn't seem concerned that the fern was ugly. Months went by, and Brenda's affection for the plant grew even when the fern's leaves did not. The plant was deeply confused and didn't know what to do with its resentful feelings. It started flinging its invisible energy over Brenda when she entered the reading room. It would wrap its energy around her like invisible tentacles and scour beneath her joy for malicious motive or evil intent while Brenda watered it. It found nothing. She was merely happy that it was healthy; her kindness had no ulterior motive.

Brenda was kind a lot actually, and the plant understood the idea of kindness less than cruelty. Morning, day, and night, Brenda would prepare large meals that the man-human and two offspring would eat away from her. She did all that work and yet was only left with one plate of food matter to nourish herself. And what did she get from them in return? Positive words, like "thank you" and "love you." Of what value were those? The plant almost felt sorry for her, except that she would wake up and happily do it again the next day.

The fern decided to take advantage of this apparent weakness. Because Brenda was no longer a threat, one by one, it allowed its leaves to curl open to take in the sunlight. With its newfound beauty also came Brenda's compliments. Surprisingly, the fern quite enjoyed them. Though at first conflicted by this, it resolved that it did not need to like Brenda to enjoy the things she did for it, so it was also not troubled when Brenda began stroking its leaves — something that used to send horror through the plant, now brought... comfort.

It became a routine for Brenda to come in and spend time talking to the plant. One special day Brenda even gave it a real name.

"Little Guy, you're not so little anymore. It's time to give you a name. Let's see... I'd say you look like a George. How do you like that name, George?"

The fern wasn't opposed to the name. It would have been happy with any name. What mattered most to the plant was the underlying intent beneath the name: it wasn't just a houseplant anymore; it was something to someone. And George enjoyed the feeling of importance very much.

Sometimes Brenda's obnoxious man-human would rudely interrupt their time together. He would barge into the room while Brenda was giving George attention and wrap his arms around Brenda, squeezing her more fragile frame. The fern smelled the oxytocin secrete from his human pores. George took all this to be some human display to keep Brenda subservient to him, and George did not like it.

The man-human would say things like, "Brenda, you weirdo, why are you always talking to that stupid houseplant?" George worried that if he said "stupid houseplant" to her enough, she would be forced to feel the same way. The man was much bigger and stronger than her, after all. He could probably squeeze her to death if she did not agree. But Brenda always laughed off his jibes, wriggled out from his arms, and never let it phase her. She never gave off any signs of being threatened by man-human; and man-human strangely always radiated a respect for her despite her much smaller stature. That all got George to thinking: maybe Brenda's kindness didn't make her weak after all.

The plant started paying closer attention to her peculiarities with more wonderment than judgement. It was particularly fascinated by her feelings for her offspring. They were less than half her size, yet she loved them more than herself. This might have made sense to the plant if she had produced them asexually and were miniature replicas of herself. But the offspring only had half of her likeness inside of them, the other half came from the wretched partner of hers.

THE HOUSEPLANT

The houseplant had known Brenda's patterns for some time, but now began anticipating them. For instance, George knew that once Brenda was done making the human morning meals, that meant she would come up and give George its sweet sweet water. It anticipated the wetness, the taste of the minerals. And after its thirst was quenched, it would enjoy Brenda's attention as an after-meal snack. With the fern's happiness grew its fronds. The other women in the book club began to notice. They started to compliment George, too. (And no one tried to plantnap it, which George thought was good.)

"And that's how me and George met, right George?" Brenda's energy went from excitement to serenity as she wrapped up her story.

The plant felt the relief of the other members who had heard the story so many times before; the story might annoy them, but they still cared for her. That was the power its human, Brenda, had. George felt a secret pride. If only these woman-humans knew the real story: how a houseplant came to tolerate its human.

Now that the book club was over, Brenda waited for the last woman to go, then she sat on the window pane next to her fern and petted it like she always did when they were alone.

"I really am so grateful we found each other, George."

But this time, what she said didn't feel good to George. Something was amiss. It could feel the vibrations of pain in her fingers, even before she felt it herself.

Brenda winced and massaged her temples, trying to push the pain away. She picked up a glass of water as she cupped the side of her head.

"Where'd this headache come from?" she asked herself. "Not enough water, I suppose."

Wrong.

Hydration was definitely not her problem. The headache was her body warning Brenda that a vessel had burst and blood was flooding into her brain. The fern released its own warning into the air, which she also dismissed as she brushed away stray droplets of water from her chin. "That's better," she mumbled.

It was not.

Brenda dropped the glass. It crashed to the ground and exploded into shards that flew through the room. Then Brenda dropped on top of them. George knew the shards were painful, saw the blood they brought, but Brenda released no pain signals. Instead, the houseplant noticed a strange pulsing energy coming from her.

The plant panicked; the man and the offspring were not home to help. But through the window the plant could sense the neighbor-woman-human gardening next door. The woman-human had a spare key. But how to call her over?

The fern tried to convince the blades of grass beyond the window to transmit the message that Brenda, its human, was in danger. At first, the blades of grass ignored the fern. They disliked humans, always chopping them down before they had the opportunity to seed. But the fern persisted and eventually the blades relented. They passed the message across the yard, through the underground mycelium root-network. The roots of the roses received the message and wafted a floral translation into the air that was blown by the wind right into the gardener-woman's nose.

Because intuition comes to humans in whispers,

THE HOUSEPLANT

the floral aroma just smelled like another day amongst her roses. But this time the fragrance was laced with a message: "George's human is in danger."

The gardener-human dropped her gardening tools. She couldn't explain it, but she had a gnawing feeling that something was wrong at her neighbor's house. Though hesitant, she walked over to Brenda's and knocked. No answer.

By this time, so many of the plants of the neighborhood had received George's message through the underground network, including the large oak tree, that a cocktail of fragrances swirled around the gardner like an invisible cloud; she did not hesitate unlocking the door with her spare key and running up the steps, where she found Brenda's lifeless body.

Eventually, strangers came, carefully walked around the glass, and carried Brenda's body away. George knew she was gone forever — it understood death had taken her. But it chose to do what humans do and force that knowledge away.

The plant woke up the next morning hoping to hear Brenda's laughter downstairs. But there was no laughter and no Brenda. Days turned into a week, and there was not one sign of her. Without her warmth, mornings turned to fighting matches between man-human and two offspring. The offspring were upset. Man-human didn't cook the same food-matter Brenda did, and then he started putting her possessions in boxes.

If I grow even more beautiful, the fern thought, *that will surely bring her back, to compliment me and touch my leaves some more...*

So for two weeks the fern grew an unprecedented amount; its fronds became even more lustrous. The fern would have been considered breathtakingly beautiful to anyone who would have entered the room. If anyone did. With Brenda gone, the women's book club didn't come by, and the family members avoided the room altogether. George was alone in its beauty. Alone and thirsty.

The fern hadn't been watered in almost three weeks, and the growth spurt had used up the remaining moisture in George's soil. One night, after the plant had shut down its photosynthesis and was resting, it heard the sprinkling of water. Its first thought was Brenda had returned to water it. But it was rain pouring from outside the window. George felt how refreshed the plants were by the downpour. Its leaves felt the coolness of the droplets running down the glass; the water was right there, but on the other side of the window.

George began to wilt.

The drooping worsened the next morning. The soil around its roots was hard like rocks. Instead of nourishing George, the dry soil now sucked the remaining moisture from its roots. George began shutting down some of its systems, in hopes of conserving the wet chlorophyll that remained in its veins.

The fern's leaves went from their beautiful hue of green to yellow — to brown. That's when the man-human took notice; he walked by, stopped and came into the reading room to stare at the dying houseplant. He was carrying a large box in one hand and a glass of ice water in the other. The man-human set the glass of ice water next to George as he packed up Brenda's books from the bookshelf. Though George did not like the man-human, it was so thirsty that it let go of its pride and tried in its way to ask the man-human for water.

THE HOUSEPLANT

The man-human paused from packing to take a drink of water. He looked at George and for a moment it seemed as though he would pour some water for the plant to drink. However, the man placed the glass back down. He walked George over to the trash and tipped its pot over so that the shriveled fern slid from the pot into the darkness of the trash can. George wasn't angry at this; it understood. Humans love beauty, and who could love George now that George was ugly? Only Brenda, and she was gone.

The plant mourned in the darkness. Not because it was dying, but because it missed all the things it got from being alive. It missed Brenda watering it, it missed Brenda's compliments, It missed Brenda's touch, but most of all, it realized it missed Brenda. Even if she came back and didn't give it any of the things it most enjoyed — even if she left it there in the trash to rot, the plant would still have been happy just to hear her laugh once more.

"Tyler, take out the trash in your mother's room," George heard the man-human say.

Maybe to end in the reading room is better, the houseplant thought. And the houseplant made peace with the darkness.

"Tyler, are you taking out the trash?

"In a second, dad!"

The plant didn't notice the light of the reading room turn on, nor did it notice Brenda's little boy-offspring looking down at its dried up body; it was that far gone. Had the offspring tied up the bag, George would have been none the wiser. But the offspring didn't. His tiny hands reached into the trash and pulled George out by its dry potting soil and held it in his arms like a baby. The loving tenderness from the offspring's touch brought George back — just a little bit. And for one brief moment, there in the offspring's arms, George sensed Brenda.

"Tyler, now, please!" his father hollered from downstairs.

"I am, dad!"

The little boy-offspring took George to his room where he repotted the fern and placed it by his window. The new location was good, but George didn't like being out of the reading room that it associated so closely with Brenda.

Every morning before he went to school, Brenda's boy offspring would spray the dried-up fern and say, "You're safe now, George." Once done, he would pet the fern. Though it was too dried-up to feel the touch, the sentiment behind the touching motivated George to persist. It hoped that soon it would be well enough to be placed back in the reading room where it could keep waiting for Brenda's return.

George enjoyed listening to boy-offspring's school adventures, who his mortal enemies were for the week, and on which girls he had secret crushes. Those nights the boy cried in bed missing his mother, George would wrap its energy tentacles around him like a hug, and the boy would calm and drift off to sleep. Like the boy-human, George missed Brenda, and always would, but it realized it no longer missed the reading room. It enjoyed the bedroom and being able to sleep so close to boy-human. He was no longer just an extension of Brenda to George, but a special human being in his own right. So much so that George stopped thinking of him as "boy-offspring" and "boy-human" at all, and started thinking of him as Tyler.

One day while Tyler took care of George, the

THE HOUSEPLANT

older girl-offspring snuck in unannounced. Tyler attempted to hide it, but the fronds were poking out on either side of him.

"Isn't that the houseplant dad threw away?"

"Please don't tell," he pleaded. "I'm trying to bring George back to life."

Girl-offspring rolled her eyes and scoffed, but she didn't tell her father.

Every day she'd come in to mock her boy sibling for trying to revive "something so obviously dead" but George sensed a sincerity sprouting from the girl-offspring's habitual teasing, that blossomed into full-fledged affection for George the day Tyler pointed out a spot of green on the fern that had not been there before.

"Look Lindsay, we're bringing George back to life."

It was true. George rather liked the girl-offspring and began associating her by her human name, too. Tyler and Lindsay continued to encourage the chlorophyll to flow back into George's veins, which, in turn, brought laughter back into their throats. The laughter of the human children made George's leaves tingle, until the bedroom door burst open.

"The plant is dead. Throw it away!"

Both Tyler and Lindsay turned to see their father standing in the doorway. Apparently their laughter had drawn his attention. The man-human tried to snatch George away from Tyler, but Lindsay grabbed it first and held it away from her father. "Mom would have wanted us to keep him alive!"

The man-human stumbled backward. He didn't cry, but George sensed his sadness. Without another word, he nodded and left the room.

But the man-human, whose human name was Bill, returned to the room every day forward and asked his offspring how the "stupid houseplant" was doing. Eventually the day came he didn't need to ask — he could see it for himself. George was beautiful.

That day, he stood silent at the door quite some time before he spoke. "Your mom would be so happy to know you saved... George," he said. "You can put him back into the reading room. I'll make sure he's taken care of from here on out."

George didn't want to be away from Tyler and tried in its plant way to tell Tyler so. Tyler thought a moment before he responded to his father. "I don't want to take him back to the reading room, if that's okay. George is my friend."

So in Tyler's bedroom, George remained. The offspring took good care of the houseplant and George showed its love the only way it knew how: it grew and grew and grew. Tyler grew, too. And every year, on Tyler's human birthday, he received new plants to take care of. Over the years, his room became a menagerie of plant friends for George to talk to. George enjoyed them all but developed a particular fondness for the plant directly next to it — a palm tree it named Brenda.

The Houseplant Merch

teespring.com/the-houseplant-merchandise

As an author, I am reader-supported. When you purchase through my links, I may earn an affiliate commission. This means I will earn a small percentage on sales with no extra cost to you and in some cases, you might even get a discount from using my links.

Enjoyed the Houseplant?

YOU MIGHT ALSO LIKE ...

"The Gatherings were supposed to bring world peace. What they brought was the apocalypse."

AVAILABLE ON AMAZON

amzn.com/B08DSYPG8H

Also By

Thank you for reading *The Houseplant*. Here are my upcoming short stories that are coming out soon.

The Gatherings *horror*

The Gatherings were supposed to bring world peace. What they brought was the apocalypse.

Petrified Women *horror/thriller*

He's a jokester. He's a prankster. But is her boyfriend also a murderer?

Gertrude Dies *dark comedy*

We all die in the end. But for Gertrude, it's just the beginning.

Updates on these and other releases can be found here:

landing.jeremyraystories.com/releaseupdates

Want to read my books before anyone else — for free? Here's more about my exclusive Alpha Readers Program.

landing.jeremyraystories.com/alphareaders

Words From the Author

If this was your first time with one of my stories, thank you for reading — I hope this is just the beginning!

As my regular readers already know, reviews are really helpful in spreading the word about my work. If you enjoyed this story, you can help me by leaving a **quick review** wherever you bought this book and on **Goodreads**. A sentence or two makes a world of difference. Every review helps me move up the ranks and allows me to continue doing what I love.

Bonus

You can listen to me read **The Houseplant** on my podcast, ***Nobody Reads Short Stories.*** (Forgive my attempt at a southern accent.)

Podcast available on all major streaming services.

- Spotify
- Youtube
- Amazon Podcast
- Apple Podcast
- Stitcher

Contacting Author

I also love hearing from you!

Send me pictures of your plant babies! And if you do any social media posts pertaining to this story, please let me know! **I love re-posting and giving shout-outs to my readers.**

You can either email me at **info@jeremyraystories.com** or **tag and message** my social media handle so I don't miss the post!!!

Connect with Jeremy:

www.jeremyraystories.com

- instagram.com/jeremyraystories
- goodreads.com/jeremyraystories
- facebook.com/jeremyraystories
- twitter.com/ray_stories

Acknowledgments

Mark, thank you for going on more than one date with me, that was super nice of you. Also, thank you for always being there to listen to one of my stories.

Mom, some moms like things just because their child created it. That was never you. Thanks for always being honest; it made me work harder on my stories.

Moni, you're the best godmother ever. You've always gone above and beyond your title. (I was wondering why *The Gatherings* was selling so well in Germany then I found out you bought them all.)

Mark, Maureen, and Kyle: thank you for being so supportive. I'm so glad I know each of you.

And to my readers: most authors have to stay in one genre to please their readers. Thank you for jumping genres with me and following me wherever I go.

∽

I also have the most wonderful team that helped me put this book together. Huge thanks to: Diana Keeler, for being the best manager ever. Chelsea Everly, her input on my work, even all the way back in high school and undergrad, has been invaluable. Chris Adams, for his fast turnaround time and wonderful copy-editing. (Both my editors, Chelsea and Chris, were close high school friends, how cool is that!?) Megan Morrison for being like a godparent to my stories. Lance Buckley for a beautiful book cover. My Studio City Writer's Group for always having the most insightful notes.